GAME OVER
MAXWELL CLAY

ILLUSTRATED BY **Alegria & Omayra Michael**

Young Authors Publishing

Young Authors Publishing
www.youngauthorspublishing.org

Book Design by April Mostek

Our books may be purchased in bulk
for promotional, educational, or business use.
Please contact Young Authors Publishing by email at
info@youngauthorspublishing.org.

This book belongs to

_____

DEDICATION

This book is dedicated to my amazing family and my mentor, Ms. Brooke.

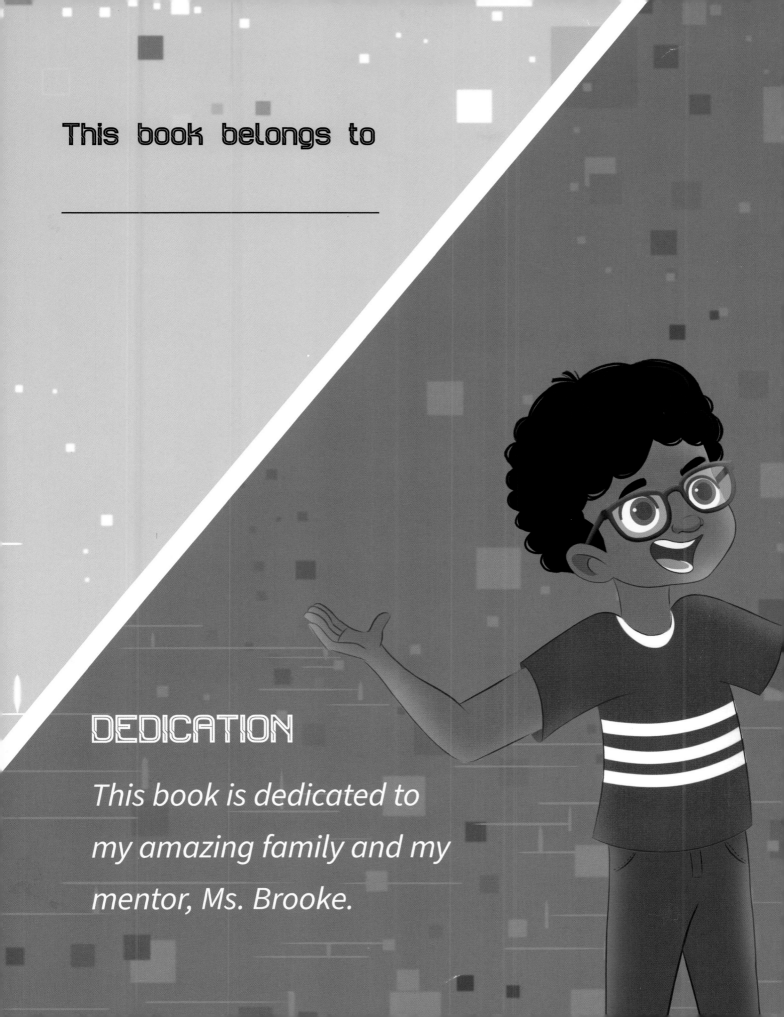

Dear Diary,

Today started off as a normal day... well, so I thought. I was sucked into my computer game in order to teach me the importance of my family and friends. Here is how it happened...

I used to spend a ton of time on my computer and TV.
When I say a ton, I mean **A TON!**

I watched YouTube videos and played my Minecraft and Fortnite video games all day. I loved to play my favorite game, GAME OVER, using the gaming headphones my mom bought me for my birthday.

One day, I was sitting in my room while playing Minecraft on my computer when my mom called me downstairs for dinner with my family.

"Honey, dinner is ready," she said. But I was in the middle of gaming and I did NOT want to stop playing. So, I said…

I even skipped my virtual 6th grade classes so that I could play! Even though I could hear my teacher calling my name, I would ignore him and continue to play my games. Isn't that crazy?!? All I ever did was play with my technology and nothing else.

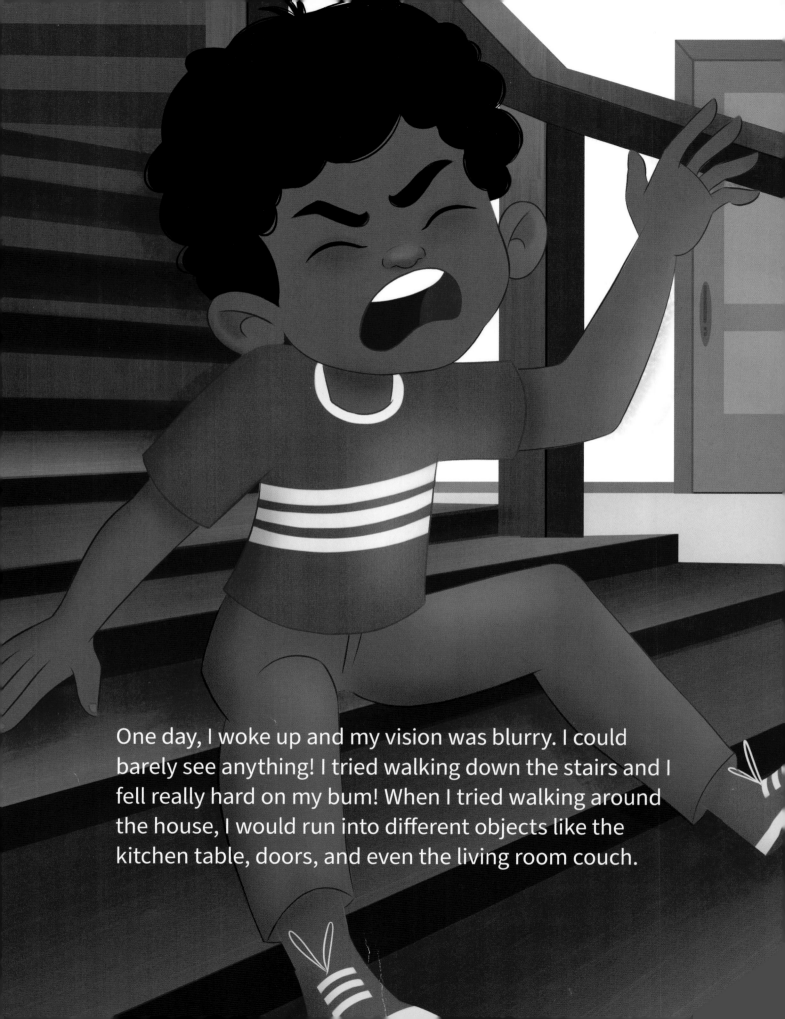

One day, I woke up and my vision was blurry. I could barely see anything! I tried walking down the stairs and I fell really hard on my bum! When I tried walking around the house, I would run into different objects like the kitchen table, doors, and even the living room couch.

In order to help me see better, my mom gave me these super cool blue glasses. She told me that I have to wear them all the time to be safe!

After getting my blue glasses, I went downstairs to get dinner, which was Hawaiian pizza! When I got downstairs, I saw that my family was playing Uno. My younger sister Addison asked me to play, but I yelled, "NO, I don't want to play with you losers." Instead, I went over to play my favorite game, GAME OVER, on the family TV.

After a while, my family went upstairs to go to bed. I continued to play GAME OVER and eventually lost the game. I got so upset that I walked up into the TV and hit it.

But something crazy happened…I got sucked into the game!

When I woke up, I didn't know where I was! I looked out and saw something familiar, my living room couch! Surprisingly, it looked so much bigger than usual. I turned around and saw two huge words floating in the sky. "GAME OVER," I read and I realized I was in my video game! My eyes got big and I began to sweat. *This can't be happening!*

I took off my blue glasses to see if maybe I was dreaming. I wasn't! I couldn't see anything without my blue glasses and that's when I realized that everything was real.

All of a sudden, I heard banging from the outside of the TV. I turned around and saw my mom pounding her fists on the TV screen. I couldn't hear her, but I could see that she was yelling my name. "Mom! Help!" I exclaimed. By looking at her face, I could tell she was really worried. But then, I didn't see her anymore!

"Alex!" I turned to my right and there was my mom inside the game with me!

As my mom and I were hugging, my blue glasses began to beep and flash really loudly. I started to walk forward and my glasses began to beep and flash even louder! I continued to walk and saw a dark cave. I couldn't see anything, but my mom said, "Look closer! I see Uno cards!"

And she was right! The Uno cards were floating right above a strange man.

"In order to pass me, you must beat this game. The first player to get rid of their deck of cards wins."

My mom ran past me and yelled, "I got this, Alex! Me, your dad, and Addison play this all the time."

I sat next to my mom as she played Uno against the strange man.

As my mom played Uno against the strange man, she said, "UNO," and had only one card left. "This is the card that always beats your dad," my mom said as she leaned over and showed me a green +2 card!

The strange man placed down a green card with the number 3. "I WIN!" my mom shouted as she put down her last card.

"Good job, Mom! I wish I knew how to play," I said, and the dark cave disappeared from around us.

My mom and I began walking when my blue glasses started beeping and flashing again! My mom tapped my shoulder and said, "Alex, look up! There is food floating around us!"

While looking at the floating food, we saw strange figures appear that looked just like Addison and my dad! A loud voice appeared and said, "Match the food and the figure who likes it correctly in 1 minute and you will win. If you lose, you will be stuck in GAME OVER forever!"

"Mom, I got this," I shouted as I brought a juicy, vegan burger up to the figure of my dad. But my mom yelled and said, "Alex, wait! Addison likes vegan burgers."

As I set down the vegan burger, my mom said to me, "Let me take over, kiddo." She brought the vegan burger to Addison's figure, Hawaiian pizza to my dad's figure, then vegan mac n' cheese to Addison, and Rocky Road ice cream to my dad! My mom was getting all of them right!

With only 30 seconds left, my mom kept matching the food to everyone perfectly! While bringing some broccoli to Addison's figure, my mom shared, "Broccoli is Addison's favorite dinner vegetable!"

Suddenly, I realized how much I didn't know about my family. With all of the time I spent playing my video games, I finally understood that I was missing out on quality time with them.

A buzzer went off and the loud voice reappeared saying, "You're lucky you won this time." My mom embraced me in a hug and I began to cry.

I felt so disappointed that I didn't know my family's likes or dislikes. My mom lifted my face and asked, "Alex, what's making you cry?"

"I'm sad that I don't know much about you, Dad, or Addison. I realize that I need to spend less time playing my video games and more time with you guys. What if I only spent two hours a day on my video games instead of all day?" I asked.

"Alex, it makes me so happy to hear you say that. All we want is for you to spend quality time with us. I think two hours a day is an awesome plan, bud."

All of a sudden, my blue glasses began to beep AGAIN and a portal to our family living room appeared! "Mom, that's our living room couch!"

"I think this is our way out! Let's run," said my mom, and we began to run toward the portal as fast as we could. I looked behind us and saw that everything in the game was fading away.

The floating food, the strange man, the Uno cards, everything!

I said to my mom, "We have to hurry and jump so we won't get stuck in the game!"

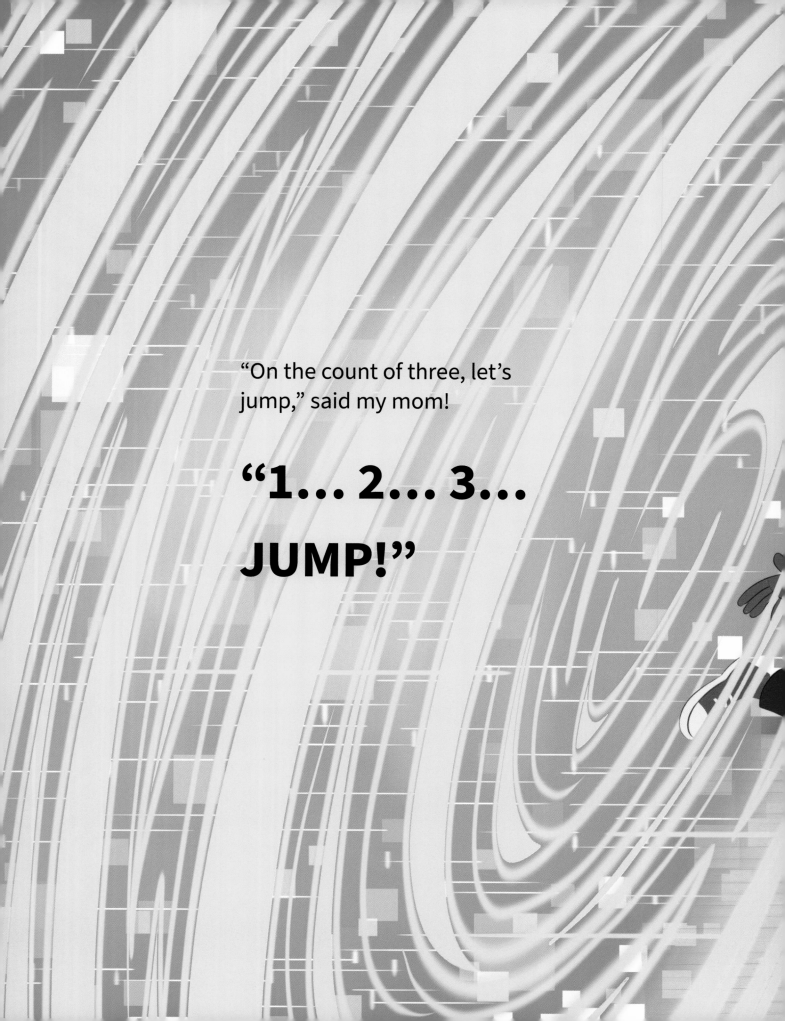

"On the count of three, let's jump," said my mom!

"1... 2... 3... JUMP!"

I woke up feeling the fuzziness of my family's living room couch, but I couldn't see! Then, I felt someone handing me a pair of blue glasses. I put them on and my vision was clear again! In front of me was my mom, my dad, and Addison.

"What happened to you guys?" my dad asked.

My mom and I looked at each other and both said, "A LOT!"

With my family all around me,
I told them, "I love you guys."

"We love you too, Alex."

And that's how I learned that my family is more important than any of my video games... even GAME OVER..

ABOUT THE AUTHOR

Maxwell Clay is 10 years old and is in the 4th grade. He enjoys playing baseball and soccer, and he loves to draw in his free time. In the future, Maxwell hopes to use his skills and talents to help individuals without homes all around the world.